FOR JADE
K.S.
FOR TIMO + MARIIKKA
L.M.

Historical Notes

Christ's birth has been associated with the appearance of a special star since His coming was prophesied during the time of Moses, and the Gospel of St. Matthew contains the account of the star that led the Wise Men to the stable in Bethlehem. Praised in many hymns and carols, a shining star is one of the most revered symbols of Christmas celebrations today.

The tradition of Christmas gift giving can be traced back to Saint Nicholas, a fourth-century bishop, whose love of children and penchant for anonymous gift giving inspired various European "Father Christmas" legends during the Middle Ages. Celebrations of *Sint Nikolaas* or *Sinter Klaas* were brought to America by Dutch settlers in the early seventeenth century.

Lapland is a vast region of northern Europe lying mostly within the Arctic Circle. Reindeer herding has been the major occupation of its people since well before the time of Christ. To this day many Laplanders lead a nomadic lifestyle, carrying tents and possessions on sleds as they follow the herds on their seasonal migrations.

First published in the United States 1998 by Dial Books • A member of Penguin Putnam Inc.
375 Hudson Street • New York, New York 10014 • Published in Great Britain by Magi Publications
Text copyright © 1998 by Kenneth Steven • Pictures copyright © 1998 by Lily Moon
All rights reserved • Printed in Belgium by Proost N.V. on acid-free paper
Library of Congress Catalog Card Number: 97-51613 • First Edition • 10 9 8 7 6 5 4 3 2 1

THE
BEARER
OF GIFTS

by Kenneth Steven
pictures by Lily Moon

Dial Books New York

In the very far north of the world is a place called Lapland. And there—where winter days are almost as dark as night and the snow is at least six feet deep—lived a lonely wood-carver.

All winter the man worked by candlelight, carving useful things. Then he would sell them, traveling across the countryside on a sled pulled by reindeer.

One night as he was fetching water from
the icy stream, the man looked up and saw
a brilliant star shining in the eastern sky.
 "It is bigger than any star I have ever
seen," the man said to his dog. "I'm sure it
was not there before."

That night the man could not sleep, for the star was shining as brightly as the summer sun. It seemed to be calling to him, inviting him to follow it and find something strange and wonderful.

All night long the man carved by the
light of the star, until he had only a scrap
of wood left. From it he made a tiny star.

The next morning the man
gazed up at the dark gray
sky. The star was still there,
but now it began to move.

Quickly the man filled a sack with his carvings,
harnessed the reindeer to his sled, and followed
the star across empty lands to the east.

The star led the man through villages where
the air was warm and people spoke languages
he could not understand.

Whenever he was hungry, he was given food
in exchange for one of his useful carvings.

And still the star led him on, but it seemed
closer and ever more bright. At the top of a
steep hill the man stopped. The lights of a town
sparkled below.

The star hovered overhead, and somehow the
man knew that his journey was nearly ended.

"Now I shall find out what strange and wonderful thing has happened," he said to his dog. Filled with joy, the man made his way down the hill toward the little town.

There was noise everywhere; laughter and spicy scents filled the air. People stared at the odd traveler with his pointy shoes and curious-looking beast.

But the man didn't notice. Following the star, he made his way through the town's winding streets. At last he came upon a tiny stable.

Very quietly the man opened the door. He saw two figures standing at a manger filled with straw. And upon the straw lay a newborn baby, bathed in a golden light. The man felt so full of peace that he moved closer and knelt beside the baby. A radiance far brighter than the star above the stable shone from the boy child's face.

As the child's parents watched in amazement, a small miracle happened. From head to toe the man glowed with a great warmth, and his rough clothing became thick and soft as it turned from blue to the richest, deepest red.

"You are blessed with a very special child," the man said to the parents. "I must honor him with a gift, for I know in my heart that he shall save the world."

The man went outside and searched his sack for something to give the child. But he had traded all of his fine carvings for food. At the very bottom of the sack the man found the tiny wooden star.

"It is all I have," he whispered to the child, "but I give it in thanks for finding you. I shall never forget this night."

And gently kissing the sleeping baby's head, the man went out into the night to begin his long journey home.

The shining star had now disappeared from the sky. But as he traveled through the darkness the man did not feel lonely or afraid, because of the special child he had seen.

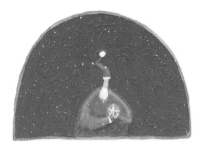

It was as if the
great warmth
he had felt were
keeping him
safe and happy
through the long
cold journey.

When the man arrived home in Lapland,
it was summertime and there were wildflowers
blooming and birds singing everywhere.

He went from camp to camp, telling the story
of the star and his journey and finding the
very special baby.

And when the days grew as dark
as night and the snow was six feet
deep once more, the man began his wood carving
again. But now he carved toys for all the children
he knew, in memory of the day he had met the
child who would save the world.

Then he packed the toys in a sack, harnessed
the reindeer, and set off on his sled to deliver a
present to every child—to those who had never
known the joy of receiving and to those who
had never known the joy of giving.

Laplanders say the man is alive to this day,
deep in a far north forest, making gifts for all
children. Some call him Father Christmas. Others
know him as Sinter Klaas or Kriss Kringle. . . .
We call him Santa Claus.